Hopeless Romantic

(A book of poems)

By Sabrina Jacobson

ISBN: 979-8-9999987-0-5

Published by: Sabrina Jacobson
Printed in the United States of America

Cover design by: Sabrina Jacobson

Disclaimer: These poems are works of creative expression. They reflect emotions, imagination, and personal growth, not literal events. Any resemblance to actual persons, living or dead, is purely coincidental. The "you," "she," and "he" in these poems are symbolic figures that represent ideas and feelings, not specific individuals.

To everyone who's still waiting to be loved,
but never stops giving it.

Author's Note:

I have always written poems, they were a way to vent; To get all of the thoughts, the good ones and the bad out of my head. I never really thought that I would make it public, but if someone here resonates with my words, then I figure it all would have been worth it. This book is not just a poetry book, it's also a way to show how much I have grown, and my journey of self-love throughout high school.

When I was 16, my dad took me to a JVKE concert for my birthday. He was my favorite artist at the time, the one who wrote Golden Hour in 2022 and was also Christian. I was in awe, seeing him live for the first time. While he was singing Moon and Back, my dad leaned in and whispered, "JVKE writes a lot of songs about finding love, maybe you should write about not finding it."Although my dad was making a joke- one that I took a little personally- it also stuck with me. I thought, *Maybe I will write about not finding love.* And now…here we are.

The truth is, I didn't have a love life in high school. Not really. A lot of these poems are dramatized-written in moments where I was trying to make sense of longing, or maybe even to imagine something I hadn't yet experienced. But even in the exaggeration, there's truth. There's feeling. And sometimes, writing about what we don't have is just another way of reaching for what we hope to find.

These collections of poems are just some of the poems that I have taken from my poetry journals throughout the years that have followed a theme: Love. Whether it be unrequited love, the hope of love, self-love, or Godly love, this is what I wanted to write about. Because the greatest thing is not just to be loved- it's to have love in your heart. To love the world and everything in it.

Hopeless Romantic

It's only in the stories
That I can fulfill my perfect love fantasy
Where all the boys I want chase me
And I am not the one
With tears falling down my cheeks

But it’s only in the stories
I guess that’s what I get
For being such a hopeless romantic.

Unrequited Love

She was light
He was darkness

He saw her,
A ray of sunshine in his eyes
When she passed by
The golden girl with a flower in her hair

He thought he was not good enough for her
His dark mind would taint her golden heart
So he thought it was better to only watch her from afar
How can light ever touch the dark?

She noticed him
Was intrigued by his darkness, his mystery
The other side of the moon she was longing to see
But she couldn't because she was blinded by her own light

When she finally reached him
She was so full of hope
Hoping her light would reach him,
Make it to the stars
But he put out the flame of her candle,
Leaving her stranded in the dark

He had a chance to grasp the light
But he chose to hide back in the night
She was left wondering if what she did wasn't right
That not everyone needs sunlight, especially him
The one whom she gave but he didn't take
And she was left alone, darkness in its wake

She knew she would never see him again
And on that final day, life tested her fate
When she looked back to see him, one last time
She realized,
He was never looking at her anyway.

Guys with Pretty Faces

Tell me why my heart beats fast
When I'm surrounded by guys with pretty faces

Tell me why I feel like I'm not the one
They end up chasing

Is he excited to see me,
Or is it just one sided?

Does he think I'm pretty,
Or am I just unwanted?

Tell me why I am like a bug spray
Keeping the guys from my dreams away

Tell me why I don't know how to talk
When he glances my way

Were you admiring me?
Or were you just looking past the sidewalk?

Am I a beacon of light, in your eyes
Or am I just someone happening to pass by?

I want to think you want me as I want you
Your smile, your laugh, I can actually call mine

But I can't help thinking I'm the latter, because if I wasn't
Something romantic would have occurred otherwise

I am in the in-between
The unsure of how I am foreseen

Is it best to know the truth,
However disappointing it would be?

Or hope that whatever you are thinking of me is the best,
Blinded by delusion and idiosyncrasy?

Just as I Admired You

Someday, I won't be just another face in the crowds
I will be the face looked for in a crowd

He'll be looking and I won't even know
He'll get weak in the knees
And he'll think, *Wow, that girl is so pretty.*

I will be the one he fantasizes,
Replays every interaction within his mind

Someday I will be the one that stands out
The one he admires from afar

The girl with a face unwilling to forget,
The girl that flowers bloom along her path and
sunshine looms above her head

One day I wonder, if I'll be the one people silently
admire,
Just as I admired you.

Pretty

I think I'm pretty
My looks are not bad
But I don't think others think I'm pretty
I wish I was the girl everyone looks at when she walks into a room
Pretty enough to turn heads
Like Taylor Swift in a music video looking like a princess
The kind that boys compare to sunsets
The kind that makes girls jealous
The kind that boys ask to dance

But instead I'm a mess
And I wish that people could see the beauty within me
But I feel invisible
Like I'm just there
A background character
I wish I could be outgoing to everybody
Not just people I'm comfortable with
Because maybe if I were cooler or prettier
I would finally be desired
I would finally find my place
And it wouldn't be so hard
To fit in with people my age

Unfinished Puzzle

I try to act put together
Make sure they don't see the unfinished puzzle
And I wait for someone to ask me
How I am doing, if I'm okay, my problems
In the back of my mouth waiting to slip out
If they ever ask

Cause deep down my heart is empty
My mind illusioned by fantasy and great
expectations
Of how beautiful I will be when I am finally
finished
But for now all I am
Is just a mess of missing pieces.

A Beautiful Dream

You were a beautiful dream.
You inspired me
To walk a little straighter, stand a little taller
I'd think about you from time to time, and wonder
What does he like?
I'd smile everytime I hear your name
And try to act cool when I see you in the hall
Whatever I achieved
I wanted you to know
In hopes that it would impress you at all

I'd post pictures and videos of myself
Just so you could watch them
And hope that you would like them
Hope that I was on your mind
Like you were on mine.

I know you never would
And that I'm probably not the only girl you think about,
But you were the only boy on my mind
Because you were a dream
Someone that makes me want to try new things
In hopes to impress you

I watch you from afar
Like that one star in the sky I can never look away from
Like a double rainbow after a hard storm
Hopefully sooner rather than later
I can make my dreams a reality
It doesn't matter how many boys I see smiling at me on the street
You were the boy I always looked back to as you passed by
You were the boy I liked
You were everything and nothing at the same time
You were a beautiful dream.

Missing

Sometimes I wish I was the only one who knew you
Because then I could show others
What they are missing

Unrequited Poem

I look at you like how I look at the moon
In the middle of the night, waking in the pool
Something so mesmerizing, like the Claire de lune
You are everything I wanted and so much more
But now I'm crying on the floor
Words of paper scattered and thrown
The bittersweet song of an unrequited poem.

The bittersweet song of an unrequited poem.

Background Character

Somebody once told me,
That I was someone who was just there
In the background
Someone you rarely think about unless they are around
And even then you never pay attention to them, because you don't care
I'm just a background character.

I pretended like it didn't matter,
But deep down it destroyed me
I still think about it as one of my biggest insecurities.

Being told that made me think
About who I am, about my place
It made me think about my friends,
About how I would rather be alone
Than just be an extra face.
How can someone say that so casually,
Like I never really mattered?

It made me believe that no one truly cared
And no matter how much I try
Deep down, I’m still scared
That I’ll always be someone who is just there.
Someone that could never be wanted,
Like the main character,
But forgotten.
Like a background character.

A Love Story

I don’t have a love story
But that's okay.
I don’t need one
I’ll put my love into other things.

But it’s still a little sad
How other people my age
Are falling in love and
I’m in my room
Writing poems at 11 pm.

It’s still a little sad that
I see couples everywhere:
At school, restaurants, vacations;
There to easily remind me,
That I don’t have a love story.

My parents say that I’m living in a different time,
That finding a guy was different
Back when they were my age,
But all it does is make me wonder
If I’m living in the wrong decade.

Because I don't just want to fall in love
But I want the hopeless romantic kind of love
The I'll follow you to the edges of the world kind of love
The I'd fall in love with you in every lifetime kind of love.

But it seems impossible
In a situationship and talking culture,
I've promised myself
I won't fall in love unless I am sure
That he is the right one.

Because I've figured
That I've waited this long for love,
Therefore what's a little more
If time measures worth?

I watch love in movies
And hear my friend's love stories
In order to live vicariously
To at least have an idea of what love could be
But all it does is easily remind me
That I don't have a love story.

Obsessed

I am obsessed with Love;
The fleeting glances, gentle touches, the beautiful words that are carved into a heart and kept there
Makes my heart want to bloom for it too.

But my heart is still a seed,
Waiting for my own love to grow

It's kind of ironic that the ones who desire love the most
Are the ones who end up being alone.

Delusion v. Reality

Sometimes I am trapped within my own mind
Creating fake scenarios in my head
Leading me to prefer my own fiction,
Rather than let reality settle back in again.

Delusional

Everytime a guy glances my way
What if it's a sign?

But at the same time, I can't tell
If he was admiring me, or not noticing

I don't pay enough attention to men
I think that in time
He'll appear in front of me and spawn

I'd like to think that there is
Some man admiring me from afar
Some man who dreams of me
Thinking of how beautiful I am

That I am the beacon of light
That I have seen the boys in my mind as,
The girl he writes poems about

Maybe, there is someone out there,
Who wants to tell me so bad
But they haven't yet

And I hope someday soon they'll have a chance
Because otherwise I will never know
And I'll continue being delusional.

The boy who came to visit me at night

There's this boy that would come to visit me at night
He'd teach me many things that my heart has never done before
He'd open up a great door
Of impossibilities

There's this boy that would come to visit me at night
He'd look at me with that twinkle in his eyes and I'd smile
Flowers in my hair,
Not a care in the world

This boy that would come to visit me at night
Would take my hand and we'd dance through life
But when I opened my eyes
The boy that would come to visit me at night
Would be nowhere in sight.

Gatsby

Five years ago,
A story untold
A man with nothing
Saved a man on a boat.
A journey he underwent,
He found his true love
But he was lost in his turmoil
He had to let her go

She was young and beautiful
Pretty like a flower
This girl called Daisy
It's quite funny
How much a woman can change a man

He waited across the bay
When he became prominent
He held parties every night
For the chance that she would stumble by
It never ceases to amaze me,
How much Gatsby loved Daisy.

But reality took its toll,
They couldn't be wild anymore
For he was a paramour
So she left him waiting
And poor Gatsby didn't know

He was lost in the past
Sometimes love collides with death
So Gatsby reached but didn't grasp
For he was shot,
And buried six feet below
Never to be reunited with his true love
From five years ago.

Shakespeare

I want to find love like the classics
Like Jack and Rose in The Titanic

I want love like Shakespeare in a sonnet
A love story as infamous as Romeo and Juliet

But God hasn't written my love story yet
For now, all I am is an unfortunate poet

Single Friend

I get it, I am the single friend.
The one who you laugh at when they sit alone
The one who doesn't do anything wrong
But can never seem to find someone

I get it.
I am the only one in the group
Who doesn't have a sickly romance
And I am the one who gets made fun of
For their "nonexistent love"
They say it's an 'achievement', not finding love this long
Yes, it's quite an achievement, being the single friend.
I get it, to you it's funny, how single I am,
It's funny being the single friend.

Third-Wheel

I'm tired of being the third wheel
The one without the one
I'm tired of the watching from afar

I wish he looked at me the way he looked at her
Basking in her perfection
I'm tired of being the bystander

Why can't I be the girl
The girl who has his eyes shine when they smile at him
The girl who makes guys like him nervous
The girl he'll choose for a very first kiss

I'm tired of the love
I'm tired of the affection
I'm tired of feeling like I have to leave because their romantic tension is too much

I'm tired of hearing my friends' stories
Of their relationships and heartbrokenness
Because I've never experienced any of those
And I'm not sure I will
I'm tired of being the third wheel
Of feeling like the unwanted one

Extinguished

Whenever something happens
And I start to see a spark
The fire gets put out
Before it even starts.

The people around me
Can build a fire so easily
But I can barely get a spark
Why is it so hard?

I've done everything
But the outcome is so disappointing
Is there something I am missing?
Is this some sick joke?

It really isn't funny
It breaks my stone, cold heart
That I can't even get a spark
Because the fire gets put out before it even starts.

The Girl He Wants

When I saw him, I used to get excited
All the little things, little interactions
I really liked him a lot
But I couldn't tell anyone
Because I am not the girl he wants

I saw him with a girl at lunch
I pretended not to care
But how could I not, when he was standing there?

Did he ever look at me like that once?
Maybe, or maybe not
I guess I'll never know, for I am not the girl he
wants

I never manage to end up in a relationship
I am not the one they tend to like
It's so hard for me to finally accept
I really thought that I had a chance
But he thinks of me like he thinks of anyone
For I am not the girl he wants

Is it impossible?
Is there something I am doing wrong?
I just can't stand, I cannot fathom
Being the girl he does not want

It never actually happened
I made a big deal over nothing
But I can't swallow my heart
When I finally accept
That I am not the girl he wants

I'd like to think
That I might meet the one
That I don't write depressing poems about
I'd like to think that when I see him again
Time will exact my revenge
I'll go from being the girl he does not want
To the one he wants but cannot have

But until time is by my side
I'll have to finally accept,
And live with the fact
That I am not the girl he wants.

Excited over Nothing

Whenever someone seems to show interest
I always end up thinking,
Could it actually happen?
And I get all excited
I start daydreaming

And I count the days until it happens again
But I find myself waiting for him
And days turn into weeks
The moon changes its phases
And I end up losing hope, it was all pointless

How stupid of me was it to think
That the thing that I dream about so often would
suddenly happen?
I am so naive
I am just a girl wanting to love and be loved in
return

How stupid of me was it to think
I was all excited
Only to realize it didn't happen
I was all excited over nothing.

Hopeless Love

Whenever she saw him, her face would light up
Her eyes would sparkle like the stars
And she'd daydream of him everyday

He never noticed that special sparkle
Or the way her dimples curved when he looked at her
He never bothered to truly look at her

And overtime,
That sparkle died.
That sunshine started to fade
Until the hope truly went away

She moved on.
And her sunshine lit up a different boy's day
And that's when he realized
The priceless gold that he threw away.

Not Your Type

I used to think the world of you
Think of you so highly
I thought you were so nice
But you say I'm not your type

You say I'm not your type
I die a little inside
Because deep down I wanted to hope
That a part of you would like me too

You say I'm not your type
Or was it a lie
So you wouldn't admit that I'm the one you like
I wish that was it, but I think we both know the truth

You say I'm not your type
I guess you really were just being nice
And now I can finally move on to another guy
Who I will also never be able to call mine

You say I'm not your type
I didn't take you to be the superficial kind
I guess I was just another admirer
You'll find love in another

You were just another crush
Never to be my first real love
I wish just once
That I could be the girl
That the guys I pine for would admire
I wish I was your type

Happy Crush

I am looking for love
But can never seem to find it
And everything seems to show
That guys don't like me enough
I'm just a happy crush
One they are content with seeing everyday
Or whenever I pass by their way
But not enough of a crush to get to know,
Not interested enough to get ahold.

My heart is disappointed, and broken in two
That I seem to be the girl that guys like,
But don't like enough to pursue.
And I wonder why the world could be so cruel
To have every guy I like be one sided
To have every miniscule chance I have at love to be unrequited

And deep, deep down I'm afraid
That I'm not worth it in guys' eyes
To be the one they'd like
The one they'd like enough to be able to commit fully

So I go at it alone
Because it is not worth it
If I am just a happy crush
To be admired by silently
But not enough to make a guy fall in love
Or to even try.

Stories

I don't have to have friends
It would be nice but I don't need them
I know that if I build a beautiful garden for myself,
the friends will come and go

I don't have to find love
It would be nice but I don't need it
I would rather wait for that beautiful butterfly to
come,
Because if I'm going to be honest, I'm rather picky
I think that most guys don't deserve a girl like me
I wait for my love in stories
Being that vulnerable, that open, is rather scary
So I'll stick to my love in stories

The main characters in the stories I read, I find are
just like me
They don't have many friends
They are in a battle between
And they don't need anyone else
For they are the hero of their own story

Unlike me however, they have the perfect man to fall for them
I want a love exactly like that
And until it happens and God allows it
I'll hide, and abide my time,
Leading a happily ever after
Inside of my stories

Written By A Woman

He's perfect
Just for me
He looks at me like I am the world, his life
And that he'd die if anything ever happened to me

He writes me poems
And sings me songs
And buys me flowers, my favorite flowers!

He knows that I fiddle when I'm nervous
And can feel so alone in a crowded room, but at
ease when it is just us two
He has this smile that gets me weak in the knees
And I am the name he mutters in his dreams.

I'm in love with him
I'm in love with him
I'm in love with this man,
But he was written by a woman.

Once Upon A Broken Heart

Once upon a time
A girl risked it all
For the boy she loved
Only to end up with a broken heart

Once upon a time
A boy was destined to fall in love with a fox
And wear many battle scars
No one could heal his heart, or so he thought
But then came the girl with a broken heart

He watched her suffer
Through curses and through fire
Just like he did at one time
And he held her tighter, for he would rather burn
Than watch her die

And that's when she knew
That he was the one to mend her heart
The boy of apples and arrows
But little did she know
He gave up before he tried
For he feared she was the fox, who in his arms would die

She stood up tall, her heart full of hope
Wondering if it will be enough
To break the curse, and be in love
Instead of facing the tragedy countlessly foretold.

Prince

A heart of gold
And a smile that is bright
Eyes that give off an ethereal light
Hair that flirts with the wind
And a voice that melts the stars
He is so radiant, how could he ever notice me?
But he will!
He will notice me!
He will look at my soul, my eyes, and my smile,
And shine like no boy has before,
And we'll brace ourselves of what's to come,
And fall in love.

He noticed me!
He smiles at me, and admires me up close and afar!
I smile back at him, and when he looks at me, I
think the world is going to end.
I finally have him, I have my prince, the one I have
been waiting for!
And it is everything I have dreamed of and so much
more.
And that's where our story begins.
Well, that's how it would begin,
As soon as it happens.

Beautiful

My faults are my own
Each day I'm struggling to cope
And I feel so alone,
Like I'm the only one who can barely stay afloat.

I cry my mascara away
Dreading the problems I have to face
Seeing my ugly truth
In the mirror everyday
And people tell me success takes time,
Don't worry, I know I'm beautiful,
I'm just the messy kind.

Fantasy

Haunted by romanticism
And reaching for the key
A fool of optimism
Driven into ecstasy

Where is the phantom
I have sculpted so carefully
Where is this dream
That was glorified by a fantasy?

In Her Dreams

In her dreams, he smiled
In her nightmares, he smiled
She couldn't tell the difference between
Whether he wanted to hurt her or love her
But the sad, lonely little girl cried out
And she started to wonder, dreams or nightmares
Which were better

Alone

I've always been alone
Hiding behind words, books, lyrics, and poems

Thinking that love is not something for me
It could never be achieved
Move on to some other dream
Because love was never meant for me

I've been told what love is
"Just wait till someone breaks your heart."
I've already had my heart broken
By the impossibility of me finding love
How does one's heart break, if they've never had
someone to break it?

I've picked up the pieces myself
Viewing love from a looking glass
Seeing it so close, but also so far
Like how one looks up and sees the stars

Love is my reflection
Something that looks real, but it isn't
Something that seems like you can touch,
When in reality it's just a hallucination

So I walk with my head down
My nose in a book
And my heart closed
Because it was never open anyway
I've only ever loved in books
I give my book-shaped heart away
But never do I know
If my real heart will be given someday

I don't know how the world is seen
When one special person makes your heart gleam
Someday maybe, or maybe not
I don't know if God has somebody for me to love
I don't know what to do with my heart
So I keep it closed
Because that's all I'll ever know
And I wouldn't tell the difference
Because I've always been alone.

All for Nothing

You are like the breath of the wind
But when I inhale the air
I find out I'm suffocating

When all is done,
And you are gone,
I enjoy the thought, the realization,
That it was all for nothing.

Whatever will Happen to Us?

You can't get back passing time
You can't regain what is lost
And when we look back on our lives
Whatever will happen to us?

Fool about Love

My father would tell me
That the reason why I was having no opportunities provided for me,
No chance at falling in love
Was because I didn't put myself out there enough

I'd always argue that I didn't know how
And that someday I'll figure it out
And when I did, I still ended up getting rejected somehow

Maybe I love the idea of love too much,
That I end up ripping my own heart out
Maybe I care about what others think too much,
And end up wearing my heart on my own sleeve
Maybe people think love is a lot more complicated
And I think it's more simple
Maybe I am just naive
A girl, no, a fool who'd dream
That she'd be enough to make a guy fall in love
Maybe I am just a fool about love.

Here

I wish you were here
To tell all my hopes and fears
I wish you were here
To smile with and laugh at jokes

I need you, I need you
But you're not here
And all I have left is an empty house, a photo, and dried up tears.
God, I wish you were here
To give me some guidance
If you were here, things would be so different

Oh how I wish you didn't have to leave so soon
Oh how I wish you would have stayed
I wish you could have stayed.

Misunderstanding?

I'm blind and delusional
But I seemed to notice you
You seem so cool, so nonchalant
It's a shame that I am not the girl you want

I think about you, what do you do when you're not in school?
Is there another girl whose heart belongs to you?
I'm not sure I'll ever know
Because you seem to be avoiding me
Saying it was all a misunderstanding
You must be laughing, thinking of how dumb I am
That you are the first boy I approached
The first to cut my wings and throw it on the road

So I will watch you from afar
In order to protect my heart
From the battles and scars
That love wants to encroach me with
Because I gamble my heart on a string
And it's crushed by the weight of a misunderstanding.

Death of a Poet

No more words are left to say,
Utter silence is left in its wake
When a poet is broken
And her final breath is taken away

No more songs are left unsang
No more final aces to play
When a poet no longer has a muse
There's nothing left to lose

So in the dawn the poet writes
Her final words unsaid
And as she faces upon death,
Only will her words be read

As she meets her grim demise, her woe is unmatched
And she accepts her fate, the world has done it
The world must face the bitter aftermath,
Of the death of a poet.

The Boys Who Made Me Cry

To the boys who've made me cry
Who were never even mine to begin with
I hope you're happy
While you're secretly causing my misery
I hope you'll never know
How much you've made my heart sore

I'll never forget the boys who made me cry
Because they have made me want to find
A boy who'll make me blush and smile
And who'll want to stay awhile

The boys who've made me cry
Have made me realize
That I need to keep my standards high
Otherwise I'll be just another crushed up lover,
tossed aside
By the boys who've made me cry.

While I eventually forget his name
I'll never forget the way I felt inside
By the boys who made me cry.

Have you ever thought of me?

I've thought of you day and night
I've thought of you when I didn't care
I've thought of you when you weren't even there
Have you ever thought of me?

I've thought of you when I was crying
I've thought of you when I was smiling
I've thought of you when I was miles away
Have you ever thought of me?

I may not be good with words out loud
But man, am I good at writing them
Sometimes I can't help but wonder
If my words were on a billboard someday
Would you ever stop and read?
Would you ever think of me?

I've thought of you when I was alone
I've thought of you when I went to sleep
I've thought of you in my dreams
Have you ever thought of me?

There Will Be Other Boys

My mind is being plagued
Because I like someone
Who I don't know
I don't know how he feels about me
And it always makes me think
That boys are so confusing

It's too late to get my hopes up, he probably doesn't like me
And I complain because it hurts to not feel wanted the way I want to be
Will I ever get over this feeling?

No other boys are on my mind,
And I can't see myself in a relationship of any kind
I tell my friends that I feel this void,
And they tell me,
"There will be other boys."

It's not my priority,
But it's always on the back of my mind,
And everyday I wonder,
Will this be the day I meet a boy I like?

But everyday is the same,
No boy has ever came,
And I sit and complain
Wondering if there will be other boys
Or if he'd change his mind
Or if I'll ever have the connection,
The love I always pine.

You

I don't want to admit it
But I still think of you sometimes
It's like my brain won't allow me to forget
And I think of how things could have been different
And I think of how things have changed since you
left

I don't know which is better or worse;
The fact that I'll never see you again
Or the fact that I'll never see you again.
But it does get less painful overtime,
And I wonder what will happen,
When you have fully left my mind
When every trace of you in my head
Has truly left.

To Love A Monster

Is it justified to love a monster?
His morals may be skewed, but the way he looks at her
The pining, wanting, for love and acceptance
Only to escape in a world full of darkness.

Is it justified to love someone with the voice of an angel, but the face and heart of a devil?
She was the angel of his eternal night, the one that gave him hope for life.
He gave her his music and wrapped it in a pretty bow with a rose.
Who would have thought that the angel of her dreams would end up being a nightmare?

Yet I can't help but admire
His pitiful desires
And I replay his tear streaked face
As he mourns his woeful fate

And the hero gets the girl, because never in the world would a villain get the girl
Never in the world, would it be justified to love a monster.

Nightmare

I thought you were a dream
But you weren't
I can't believe I wanted you
And you don't feel the same
My eyes refuse to cry
But my heart still aches
A throbbing kind of pain
But I will be okay.

What really makes me sad
Is that I thought you were a dream
But as I stood there
A dream turned into a nightmare

I know you didn't mean it
But I still feel sorry for you
Cause you were not the dream
I thought I once knew.

How to Avoid You

Each day I play a game,
A game on how to avoid you
But when I suddenly see you
I close my eyes and count to ten
And when I open them,
I hope you are out of my sight.

I pretend that you don't exist
And tell myself it's better like this
I wish it didn't have to be this way
But I am not the one to blame.

I cannot stand the sight of you
Because it hurts
And I don't know how much more of it I can take
When I see you it's like a twist to the wound
I was a fool for ever liking you.

Detach

When someone says no,
I move on and let go
I will not be stuck in the past
A realistic limbo
I am too busy to think about that
I have better plans
They will only hinder it
So I must detach

I banish you from my thoughts, from my mind
I detach you from my life
Because I am a high-value woman
And you're not worth my time

So goodbye, farewell
Maybe you'll regret it
You made a huge mistake
Or maybe not
It doesn't matter anyway.
I truly don't care
I detach you from my life.

Pain

Someone knocks me to the floor
My throat quivers, *shaking*
As I hear the laughter walk out the room
And feel the crack of my heart, *breaking*

I give someone my heart
And they tell me thanks
Without knowing that was the final card
And they just threw it away

I bruise, I scrape, I *bleed*
I fall down on my knees
My tears cascade
Watering the pages that I read
But, then I smile, I *laugh*
I move with the pain
And when I get back up
I smile, and ask God to do it again.

Just a Boy

You're just a boy
And I am a poet

Your mind is a race
While my mind is flowing

You've got the nerves
And I've got the grace
I've got the heart
But you have the spades

You're just a boy
Who can barely speak
And I am the poet
The one who bleeds

We are so evenly detached
Your heart is not aligned with your eyes
While my eyes see the blurry and clear lines

I'm driven by the hidden passion
While you follow the road that is driven

You are just a boy
But I am a poet.

Not my Fault

It's not my fault
That guys don't beg for my attention
It's not my fault
That they don't want to be my boyfriend

Yes, I may still be figuring things out
But I am happy and content with myself
Meanwhile, they are blind to see
So I remain in hiding.

It's not my fault
That I remain invisible
I am not.
Just like how people can't see the sun
Because they are too afraid to look at it
So, instead of blinding everyone,
I remain in hiding.

It's not my fault
That I have never been in love.

The girl with a crow feather in her hair

She was different from the rest
And she knew.

She was tougher than the rest
But she was lonely too.

She was faced with choices,
That could make or break her life.

Should she do what is expected,
For her people and her pride?

Or should she be free, unshackled,
And live out her wild side?

Why would she stay in a place
That wouldn't accept her anyways?
She is a beast, they would say

And she heard it everywhere
So she fought back and won,
With a crow feather in her hair.

Until she met a boy who could fly
He didn't care,
He wasn't scared of her

To him, she was just the girl
With a crow feather in her hair.

Solo

One thing I’ve learned,
Is that I don’t have to be too forward
Because if someone really liked me, I’d know
And if they don’t, I’d continue flying solo.

I know I won't always be alone
So, I figured might as well make the most of it
There is comfort in my solitude
A place that I let down my curtain

I’ve mistaken my fear for excitement
When I should’ve realized sooner
That I am not ready for a relationship
I am not ready for a commitment

I truly like being alone
I am peaceful in my room, in my home
Where I find comfort in my solitude
Where I find comfort being solo.

I'd Rather Be Alone

I'd rather be alone
Than not know who to trust

I'd rather be alone
Than have a sad excuse for love

I'd rather be alone
Than doubt myself too much

I'd rather be alone
Than to have everything be pointless

I'd rather be alone
Than be self-conscious

I'd rather not be alone,
But if that's what it takes for the right people to come
And the wrong ones to go,
I would rather be alone.

I am no Shakespeare

I am no Shakespeare
Who serves the world with artistic intentions
I serve the world for myself.

I cannot write a sonnet
I am merely a poet
My thoughts are not words but emotion

But even the greatest artists hate their work in some way;
Shakespeare pressured by the public stage
Franz Kafka drained by his life of mundane
Thinking his work needed to be thrown away

By far, I am not great.
I could not compete with poets of the age
Though I am here,
By all means
I am no Shakespeare.

The Art of Being Unnoticed

In the hustle of daily life, she is just a background character
Never standing out in someone's sight.

When people slow down for others, they speed by for her.

Other people's souls were loud and new, but hers was quiet and old.

She noticed the clouds, the grass, the cracks, the grains of sand
She noticed the eye contact shared with everyone but her,
She was like a well kept secret that went and walked alone
Because she knew, she was not something people were likely to notice,
She was dancing through the back alleyways and smiling in the dark
Because she knew her skill of being unnoticed was a work of art.

Symphony

I'm in my own little world sometimes
Dreaming of a far off land up in the mountains
Dreaming of a fairytale life
Dreaming of a prince by my side

But instead I'm standing alone on top of a crowd
Watching him play a symphony from afar
Listening to the music of my heart
I'm lovestruck by the violin strings
Wondering, if I'll ever only be watching, listening
But never playing

So I collect flowers
And smile at strangers
Becoming the love I've always wanted for me
Dreaming of the day
That my heart would be taken away
Just like the time it was taken by a symphony

Confidence

Sometimes it's easier to shrink into myself
When the world gets too overwhelming
Sometimes it's easier for me to look away
When someone looks at me
Rather than look them in the face

I struggle with interacting sometimes
And saying what's needed to be said
I struggle with thinking that people want to be my friend
I want to be the one that attracts

But does that mean I have to get out of my shell,
And be naked in front of the world?
It sure feels like it
And I can't help getting self-conscious
Projecting the way I feel to how others perceive me

But I know deep down, I am enough
I just have to show it in my outer presence
I just have to show that I have confidence.

Sometimes it's easier to be in my own little world
To be stuck in my own head
But if I do, I know I'll miss out on the chance
To give myself some confidence.

Effort

I worry about my future
Someone told me, *"You have to know your worth"*
I am one of a kind
A girl like no one has ever met before
And I want to love some more
Like how God loved the world
It doesn't hurt to try, to put in some effort

It doesn't hurt to try
To show how much I care
About the things I am willing to put effort in

The people that I like
Will turn into the people that I love
And hopefully I will be loved in return
And if not,
It still didn't hurt to put in some effort

If everybody cared so much
The world would be so full
Like a bouquet of roses with no thorns
No more blood to spill

But even as I lie
I know I’m not alone
And if I am alone, I wouldn't be hurt
Because at least I know I tried
To put in a little bit of effort

Invisible

It’s weird to think
That I am not as invisible as I thought

Its weird to think that I am the girl
Who walks through a door
And people whisper *“that's her.”*

It’s weird to think that people feel
Happy, excited, nervous
When I pass by
That they can sense my presence
Whenever I’m nearby

It’s weird to think that
I am someone that a person wants to get to know
It’s weird to think that I am not invisible

It’s weird to think that
I am someone people think of
It’s weird to think that
I am not as invisible as I once thought.

Freak?

Am I a freak?
Because I sometimes act like a child
Am I a freak?
Because I've never talked to a man
Am I a freak?
Because I've never kissed, never dated, never even held hands

Does it make me a freak,
To be alone most of the time
And laugh at my own jokes
And does it make me a freak,
That I enjoy solely my own company?

It is the way it is

Maybe I don't want the thing I wanted as much as I once thought
Because the more I think about it
The more I think I'm not ready
And I don't want it to change me
I'm so used to things the way it is
I've been on the sidelines too long
That I wouldn't even know if I was doing something wrong
I've been on the bench watching the game, but never playing

It's a shame, but that's the way it is
That I've never had a first kiss
But how do things like that even happen?
Sometimes it's better to imagine the what-if's,
The could've-beens, the somedays,
Rather than watch reality hit me like a brick
Cause that is just the way it is

Always the one watching, dreaming, listening,
Of tales of love and tragedy
But will it ever happen to me?
Or will I be stuck, watching from a window
Having the opportunities fall like snow
Touching my hand and melting as soon as it makes contact
And I watch from a distance
Dreaming of what could've been, the what-ifs
Because that is just the way it is.

Romeo

When I look at myself in the mirror,
I look good.
I think to myself, *I actually wake up like this*

But then I start to doubt
If I know and think I am pretty
Then why don't guys want to date me?
Why doesn't a cute boy ask for my number, or ask me to prom at school?
Why doesn't a guy ask me on a date, and try to woo me with flowers and chocolate?
How come I don't receive love letters, because I know that I deserve that
But as far as I know, he does not yet exist, my Romeo.

If love is such a tender thing, then one day hopefully,
I'll have a Romeo fall under my spell
And we'll be star crossed lovers throughout heaven and hell
But as far as I know
He does not yet exist, my Romeo.

The Best Thing

Call me delusional, call me crazy
But I am going to believe
The only reason he rejected me was because he liked me,
And he knew that if he said yes
He would undoubtedly fall for me
And he wasn't ready for that
So he let me go.

And I don't want to waste my time on a guy who isn't worthy of it,
Who doesn't have the confidence,
Who doesn't have his heart on God,
To love himself or anyone else for that matter.
Maybe, just maybe, that was what God was telling me.
Maybe, just maybe, rejection was the best thing.

Someday

It used to bug me, but not anymore,
That I am not a girl who's been asked out before.
I must admit, what I constantly dream about is to be
loved the way I want to be.

Where some blurry, faceless man,
Will show me a love that would be worth the wait.
I dream to have a man that makes my reality better
than my dreams.
I want to be the girl with a man where everyone
sees us and says, "*I wish I had someone who looked
at me like that.*"

Yet the more I pray
The more it seems farther away
I am at peace, but sometimes peace can be lonely
Being struck by reality
And academic validity
Burying myself in activities
So the days I spend alone won't be wasted away
And every night I wonder, I dream,
Of that faceless man someday…

Lover Girl

There is no doubt when I say
I am a lover girl,
Always have been, always will.
I am a lover girl,
A lover girl that hasn't found somebody to love yet.

Curiosity

My curiosity is entangling
And driving me crazy
Because I want to know *more.*
I don't just want a summary.

I want to know *why?*
I want to know *how?*
I want to know what could've been

But I'm not sure I will ever be answered.
And the curiosity is killing me.

What is Love?

What is love?
I often wonder,
What makes love,
Something so sought after?

Love is something that is here,
In the crevasses, in the cracks
Love is something you can hear
Hidden behind a laugh.

Love is the friendly smiles
That greet you when you walk by
Love is the hope that someone
Can mend your soul when they catch your eye.

Love is every song, every melody that has been
played,
Love is the words that I passionately pray
Each morning, night, and day.

Love is the feeling of despair
When your mind knows just how much you care
But it is also the feeling of something euphoric,
Something that makes you brighter, freer, lighter.
It is something one cannot seem to bear,
But cannot bear to live without.

Love is the breeze blowing in the air,
Love is the sun in the sky
Or the rain that taps on a window at night.
Love is the feeling every object, creature, being,
deserves to one another.

Love is something that is within us all
Therefore one cannot go by
Living a loveless life
For a loveless life is no life at all

Romanticizing

I love romanticizing things
Singing to music on late night drives
Going on a run at sunset and sunrise
Walking in the snow in the middle of the night
Listening to Lana Del Rey by the fireplace
Succumbing myself to the rhythm of jazz
While thinking about the daily dose of eye contact
Maybe I am crazy,
Maybe I am mad.
But what exactly is wrong with that?
I'm high on life
And that's all I could ever want
The main character in my own story
Oh, how I love to love
How I love to smile about anything,
How I love romanticizing things.

Beautiful (Reprise)

I'm delusional and a bit naive
I always hope for things that don't happen to me.
Yet I find myself dreaming of when that will change.
It's like I have a weird view of reality,
I want to see the best in things even if it's crazy.

Life really is beautiful, and I know I am too,
Just perhaps not in a conventional way, not in a standard way.

I am beautiful for my mind, and the shimmer in my eyes,
The eyes of a child seeing the ocean for the very first time.
I am also cloaked with hidden anxieties, hopes, and dreams
That I long to fulfill someday, so much it makes my heart ache.

Viewing life in that distorted way;
Like a nostalgic fairytale that you haven't read in years
Like a kaleidoscope, where everything is colorful and bright.
Believe me, I know I'm crazy,
I'm just the beautiful kind.

Priceless

Is there a number so huge that you can't put a word
on it?
Each star in the sky, every single creature on land
Every organism in a single cell,
Each and every grain of sand
Is so big, so vast, that it is impossible to have a
price tag.
And God, the one who created organisms,
mountains, sea, and sand, also created you.
You are made up of every single piece of God,
You are made of the mountains, stars, sea, and sand,
That He created with His own two hands.
That much effort has an immense worth,
So much that it can't be put into words or numbers.
It is so special, so valuable, so intense, it's priceless.
You are priceless.

Luck

I may be unlucky in love
But I am lucky in God.
So I don't have a luckless love, but a universal love.

Better Plan

The step I take
I thought was in the right direction
Was actually the wrong way
And I get pummeled with rejection

As I head back to the start of my path
Realizing I've never really gone anywhere
I close my eyes and listen
And know that there is a better plan for me out there.

So when love takes a toll
And I forfeit the roll
I know that each step back
Is a path in the right direction
Because there is a plan just for me
That I cannot view completely yet
God has blocked the view in progress
But I know that there is a better plan for me.

Heart

I think the heart is the most peculiar organ in the body,
But the most miraculous one.
How can it beat that long without getting tired?
How can it feel like it breaks without really breaking?
How can two separate hearts be combined
And share a life of love?
But most of all, when one's bounded heart dies,
How can the other heart go on?

His Love

Whatever cards that may be played,
I should not hold my breath.
The Lord will guide me through the game,
The game of life and death.

Don't cry, don't whine, don't complain,
About the things that you don't have
For God supplies you with what you need,
All you have to do is ask.

When I cannot see my own path,
I shouldn't worry, I shouldn't fret,
Because He is holding my hand.

He sees me cry, and He sees me smile,
And He tells me I am beautiful in every way.
Even when I disappoint Him, He greets me with
open arms,
And when I get myself in a rough situation,
He protects me from any harm.

He has been there everyday,
Here by my side and guarding my back.
Since He loves me so much,
It would be foolish of me not to do the same.

Because when you love Him,
And give to Him all that you could take,
You realize it wasn't really an option,
Because there's so much more you gain.

The Art of Waiting

The time it takes for the snow to melt
And the grass to turn green
Passes by so anxiously, so gradually,
It's so slow, the passing of time that when you watch,
When you sit and stare,
There is nothing there.

Yet, the snow does melt.
It melts and sprouts beautiful fields of envy,
Dancing up from the dirt onto the floor of soil.
But, waiting can be turmoil.
When you wait for the storm to pass, then a rainbow will come
The longer you wait for a flower to grow,
The more beautiful it will sprout
Therefore the longer you wait, the more rewarding it will be.

Waiting can be a torturous, excruciating thing.
But beautiful masterpieces are created
When you give it time to be built.
Beautiful things are given to the world,
When you give time for the snow to melt.
The next time you find yourself waiting,
Waiting for the apple to fall out of the tree
Recall that beautiful things come from waiting.

Fall in Love

I thank God for not giving me love
When He knew I was not ready for it.

And now, I accept that it will be here when God is ready for me.
But, before I fall in love
I want to fall in *love* with love.
Instead of searching for it everywhere I go,
I want to become the love, everywhere I go.
I become the love that I want for me.

Maybe, when I become the love I fall in love with,
Then I will fall in love with myself,
And I would not need any love to look for any longer.

Everlasting Life

The martyr on the cross
Died because He loved us so much
He was willing to suffer
To give everlasting life

Even when He was mocked and beaten,
He cried and asked *"Father, please forgive them"*
With a heart as open as His,
He faced the most persecution
But the highest reward in heaven

God, give me a heart as open as His,
Not for the reward
But for the gratefulness that You have a plan
That is so big most can't even comprehend
Even in suffering, prosecution, or rewards
My voice is heard
And my heart is Yours.

When the time comes

My heart is a sword
My brain is a shield
Protecting me from enemies outside and within.
Allowing me to let the walls down
For people I discern to be worthy.

When the time comes for the wall of my heart to
fall,
It will be worth every mistake I have ever made
Every choice I am willing to make
Every action I have chosen to take.
So, in patience I brace,
For when the time comes.

I am beautiful

I am beautiful
I am wanted
I am loved
I remind myself,
I don't need to compare
Because I shouldn’t care
Just be kind,
And I will attract the butterflies.

I am beautiful
I am wanted
Though I may not always think that,
There are men out there, kind and good-hearted
Who are waiting for a girl like me
I appear as the girl of their dreams

So I don’t need to compare
Because I deserve to love the world, and be loved in return.
And even if not everyone likes me that's okay.
Because I like me.
I love me.
I am beautiful.

Pessimism v. Optimism

To the ones who view the glass half empty;
The book half closed
The day is over because of the storm
The clothes are ruined because they are torn
The armor of a risky fall,
The voice that tells you,
Why try at all?
Pessimism is the frustration of a broken pen
That never lets you write or say a single word again

But to learn how to dance through the storm
To view the glass half full
To embrace the silence before a song
To transcend the stairs of your greatest dream
The dream of flying despite the fall,
Is something one day you will achieve;
It is the greatest gift of all.

Who Cares?

We spend too much time thinking of what others think of us
That we don't ever end up thinking of others

We pass the time trying to be liked
But when you do that, you never do anything for yourself.

So, who cares what they think?
Thoughts are all relative
You're never really disliked until you dislike yourself
And you are never really loved until you love yourself

So, who cares?
It doesn't matter
Let yourself be a background character
Because you are one in many stories,
But they are not yours to tell
What only matters is that you are the main character in your own,
So you have to write it well.

Unsaid Goodbyes

How many times, she wonders
How many people
Wanted to say goodbye
But didn’t have the nerve to look her in the eye
How many people have wanted to say goodbye
But were just too anxious, too scared to walk on by

But then she leaves and they realize, they missed her
And she never gets to hear those silent confessions
And she wonders, how many goodbyes have been left unsaid

And now that she's gone
It’s too late for anything to be done
The thoughts are left hanging
The words are laid for no one to see
And she wonders why,
When we have the chance we let it die
And we never get to say those unsaid goodbyes.

New Beginnings

The case is closed
The deed is done
The chapter is finished
The battle is won

And what happens next?
After happily ever after?
What happens next is what happens after the credits
die
A new story, new beginning of a life.

So now that this chapter is closed,
I keep the door warm and ready
To walk through the new beginnings.

Friends

Friends are the concrete
That fills an empty crack
They're the harmonies
That make a melody complete

Sometimes they come and go
But when they stick around
You get introduced to a whole new world
A world that's full and loud
A world that doesn't judge
Your true authentic self

Friends are the people you can laugh with in any situation
They make school feel like a vacation
They are the support that I need,
The anchor that grounds me to the sea
They're the finishing touches, the final brush strokes
That make a painting into a masterpiece
Friends are the love that makes my heart smile
And make everything worthwhile.

The Sky

I'm a "*look at the sky*" kind of girl
I love to watch the sunset glimmer over a lake
Whenever I see a bird fly by
I always wonder where it's headed

Whenever I look at the sky
Something in my mind
Tells me that everything is going to be alright.

When I look at my family
I see the sky in their eyes
And the whisper of the sky
Telling me, *"It's all going to be fine."*

Whenever I look at the sky
Whenever I look at my family
I think to myself, *How did I get to be so lucky?*
That I could find such love in my life
And the love I have for them
Is something that I could never change
Because I love them like I love the sky.

The Girl with Flowers in Her Hair

When she walks into a room
The light shines upon her face
And when she smiles, she has an ethereal glow
And everyone's eyes can't help but follow her as she goes

She walks without a care in the world
Just her, her books, and flowers in her hair
And when she walks into sight
The first thing they think is *"Where has she been all my life?"*
She's the kind of girl someone sees once but thinks about day and night

Her presence is something unwilling to forget
Because she has God's love as a silhouette
And she walks without a care
Because she is the girl with flowers in her hair

Like My Dad

I have so much love
So much love in my life
From my family, from my friends,
That romance is not needed, but it would be nice.

Everytime I cry, my mom hugs my tears away.
And when I graduate, my parents are the ones
yelling out my name.

Who needs flowers, when my parents give me roses
handpainted in gold?
And who needs chocolates, when my mom bakes
me treats that are homemade?
Who needs company, when my brother protects me
and joins me in almost everything?

I have already found the rare kind of love,
The kind that most people spend their whole lives
searching for
The kind of love that makes you want to sing and
dance
The kind of love that makes you want to scream off
the Empire State Building

So I consider myself lucky, that my dad is the only man in my life for now
Who loves me more than the stories I watch and read about
Who is proud of me, and everything that I achieve
Oh, how I dream to someday find a man like that,
A man who loves me like my dad.

Hopeful Romantic

Why do we call someone who loves romance
Who loves love, a hopeless romantic?
It sounds rather pessimistic

But being a hopeless romantic
Means that you want the best things out of life
The kind of love that shows only once in a while
Love that tests time and fate
True love, that is worth the wait

So I think it's beautiful, not hopeless
Hoping for something that is so immense
It's *hopeful,* not hopeless
It's lovely, isn't it?
Being a hopeful romantic

May we forget the rain, when the flowers come.

Made in the USA
Las Vegas, NV
21 October 2025

32598194R00069